Camp Pleasure

After our prom and graduation. My white sister Kaitlin and I were off for the summer until we both attend the university of Colorado. We currently live in Denver, Colorado with my white mommy Katherine and white daddy Kent.

All four of us were sitting on the couch watching the news. When Katherine asked if anyone wanted to go camping at camp Boom Boom. I laughed out loud, Katherine gave me the look and I stopped laughing immediately.

Katherine said so show of hands who wants to go camping with me this summer. No one raised their hands, so I said I'll go with you Katherine. She said thank you sweetheart, it's going to be a lot of fun just the two of us. I said I look forward to it.

Kent said you guys better take the rifles just in case of bears. I said definitely, Katherine said I'll get them out of the safe, clean and load them before we take off to the camp.

I am happy that Kent taught me and Kaitlin how to shoot a rifle at the local gun range. I got pretty good at it, I got a few perfect shots in, that made Kent very proud of me.

A week later, when Katherine came home from work. We packed up the Toyota Tacoma and headed up to Camp Boom Boom. I took a picture of the sign and Katherine giggled, she said very funny. I said just documenting our camping trip.

Katherine said whatever buster. When we arrived at the camp in a desire location that Katherine picked out. We set up our tent first and made sure that it was secure. I nailed the anchors into the ground thoroughly so we didn't blow away.

Katherine made us a fire and cooked us dinner. We ate and talked about a lot of stuff. When we got tired, we put out the fire and turned in for the night.

I let Katherine change first, she came out in a sexy little night gown and told me to get ready for bed. I stripped down to my boxers and said I'm ready for bed. Katherine came in looking at my body and smiling. She was the first into the sleeping bag.

I joined her in the same sleeping bag. Katherine told me to spoon her, and I did what she wanted. I held her hot body and we went to sleep. We slept for a while until I woke up fully aroused with my hard penis glued to Katherine's wonderful ass.

Katherine said what's wrong sweetheart, can't sleep. I said yeah, a boner problem. Katherine said it feels good on my big ass. I said you like it, Katherine. She said oh yeah, your big penis feels really good. I playfully banged my cock on her big ass.

Katherine said oh yeah big boy, give it to your white mommy, grab my big titties. I grabbed her big titties and squeezed them good. Katherine pulled up her night gown then she said pull down your boxers telling me that it would feel better.

I pulled down my boxers and grind my hard-black cock on her bare white ass. Katherine said oh my god this brings back memories of us dancing at the prom with you being hard all night. I said that was the best prom ever dancing with the hottest babe in the building. Katherine giggled then said you're so sweet, I was wet all night like I am now.

I said wow your wet, I reached down to feel her pussy. I pushed my middle finger into her pussy and Katherine said I told you I was wet; your long ass finger feels great in my white pussy. I said oh god this is so intoxicating. Katherine said it would feel even better if you would stick your big black dick in my white pussy and fuck me until we both have an orgasm.

I held my cock and Katherine lifted up her leg, so I get a better angle to stick my dick in her. Katherine's pussy was so tight I couldn't get it in on the first try so I had to force my dick into her little white pussy.

When I fully penetrated hot Katherine, I moaned oh yeah, I've always wanted to stick my black dick in your white pussy. Katherine said I was hoping for some of your cock since prom. I slowly fucked Katherine's tight little hole.

I fucked her tight pussy harder and harder, and Katherine told me how much she loved my big black cock deep in her white pussy. I love hearing that and I felt Katherine's pussy vibrating on my cock and lubricating it.

Moments later, I grunted and ejaculated inside of Katherine's horny pussy. She said oh yeah honey I feel your warm seed in my pussy. I said I love filling up your tight little vagina with my warm sperm. Katherine said I love being your cream pie girl.

Katherine turned around and kissed me very passionately. We massaged each other's tongues as we kissed like crazy for a while. I massaged her sweet ass while we kissed. Katherine said that was fun and I said oh yeah big fun. I have fantasized about boning you for a while and Katherine said I've been fantasizing about you fucking me since the prom.

I said my friends at the prom wondered who my hot date was, and I told them it is great to have a hot girlfriend with big tits and a juicy ass. Katherine said you're a naughty boy not telling your friends that I was your white mommy.

I said they didn't need to know that my hot white mommy is my prom date. Katherine and I talked for a little bit then went back to sleep. We woke up naked and glued to each other. I said I love waking up to a sexy lady. Katherine said it's great to wake up in your sexy muscular arms. I smiled and Katherine said oh wow your big dick is hard again.

I said it's a morning boner, I get those all the time. Katherine said oh yeah, I like that, do you want to get on top and fuck me again. I said hell yeah. I mounted Katherine and saw a big smile on her pretty face. I penetrated her tight white vagina with my hard-black penis.

Katherine held my face and kissed me with her sexy blow job lips as I started massaging her tight little pussy. She squeezed me tight as I pounded the shit out of her. She screamed yes when she came hard. I kissed her neck and fucked her even harder. She wrapped her legs and arms around me as I showed her pussy no mercy.

I moaned oh Katherine as I filled her with my warm sperm. Katherine said I can't seem to get enough of your big black cock. I said I can't get enough of your tight white pussy either. Katherine kissed me then said I'll make us breakfast. We put on clothes and went out. Katherine made us a great breakfast as I enjoyed the view of her hot body.

We ate breakfast smiling at each other as forbidden lovers. After breakfast, we went for a long hike then came back to camp to relax. We took a shower then went to sleep cuddling up. I was woken up to a warm sensation on my cock. It was Katherine sucking my cock enthusiastically. I said how about a ride sexy mama. Katherine said I love that idea, my chocolate stud. She held my black pole and slid down like a sexy firewoman. I took the opportunity to squeeze her big titties as she fucked my cock.

Katherine moaned oh baby your dick is so good to my pussy cumming all over my black penis. I said how about doggie. She said oh yeah bending over. I mounted her from behind after I smacked and massaged her sexy ass. She looked back at me as I penetrated her tight pussy again.

I pulled her long blonde hair and filled her with black cock for a long time as she came again and again before I felt that wonderful feeling in my balls. I let my love flow into sweet Katherine. She leaned down and kissed me saying, I love being forbidden lovers with my sexy black son.

I said I love having wonderful sex with my hot white mommy. We held each other and kissed when Katherine's phone rang. It was Kent calling to check in with us. Katherine said hello sweetie, we are fine, just hanging out enjoying the beauty of nature.

I was on top of Katherine as she spoke to her husband. I was turned on by the thought of it. My cock became hard again, I pushed my black cock back into her white pussy, Katherine's eyes doubled in sized as she felt my cock in her, hard again. I started fucking her slowly as she talked to her husband.

I saw her eyes roll back in her head and she bit her hand when she came on my dick again. Moments later, my balls tightened, and I ejaculated into Katherine as she talked to her husband on the phone. I massaged her big tits as I came down from the high of ejaculating in her tight pussy as she talked to her husband on the phone.

When they hung up, Katherine kissed me and said that was hot, you getting hard and fucking me while I talk to my husband. I said I love you Katherine with my dick still in her tight pussy and she said I love you too sweetheart.

We separated our hot sexual union, we held hands and relaxed. We packed up and left to go home. I massaged Katherine's big tits and sweet white thighs as she drove us home. She had a big smile the whole drive home. Kent and Kaitlin greeted us when we arrived home.

They both asked us, how was the camping trip? I said it was a great experience learning from an expert camper. Katherine giggled and said I'm happy to teach him about some good hardcore camping. I looked at Katherine and smiled, she winked at me knowingly.

We unpacked the truck, and we both took long baths. All four of us sat down to dinner with me still smitten with Katherine. Kent got a call from work; he left and went to his office. He came back and told us he was going to Japan for the rollout of the new Tundra hybrid truck.

I said bring us back some cool Japanese souvenirs and chocolate. Kent said that he would and a few days later. I took Kent to the Denver international airport along with Kaitlin and Katherine. We all told him that we would miss him for the month that he was gone. He is the North American Vice President for Toyota.

The next day I was in my room playing video games when Katherine came in wearing a short little dress to clean up my messy room. I paused my game to watch her clean up my room. She said you don't have to stop playing your game.

I said I love watching your sexy ass jiggle around. Katherine said I still can't believe you love my big juicy ass. I said it's the best ass in Colorado and she laughed out loud. Katherine was bending over getting stuff from under the bed when I saw her bare ass with no panties.

I was already hard looking at her fine ass when I got a great idea to stick my dick in her. I dropped my pants grabbed her sexy hips and penetrated her tight little pink hole with my black bone.

Katherine moaned and said oh god honey that feels so good, I've missed your cock in me, but we have to make it quick, Kaitlin is home. That is all I needed to hear; I went to town on her tight little pussy pounding the shit out of her. I saw waves of cream on my cock as I went for it. When my moment of ecstasy arrived, I embraced it fully releasing a torrent of warm sperm into Katherine.

I held Katherine's big ass and kissed the hell out of her as she returned the passion. We heard footsteps and she went back to cleaning. I went back to my video game; Kaitlin came into my bedroom and said this room looks too clean. I said Katherine is the best cleaner. She laughed then left Kaitlin and I alone saying see you guys later for dinner.

A few days later, I was asleep in my bed when I heard wake up my chocolate stud. I need you in me very badly. It was horny Katherine in need of a stiff black cock in her white pussy. I was happy to mount her and penetrate her with my black cock.

Katherine said I love you my black boy as I fucked her hard. I said I love you too my Katherine. She smiled and kissed me lubricating my cock and balls. I thought wow she was really wet and horny as shit. I held her tight and drilled her sexy ass into the bed until I filled her with my warm seed.

After I filled her up with my pleasure. Katherine said thank you sweetheart, I really needed that and I said my pleasure Katherine, I'm always happy to fuck your tight little pussy. We held each other and kissed for a while before she said I need to go back to my bed before Kaitlin catches me.

Katherine left and I went back to sleep. I was asleep when I heard hey stud wake up its Kaitlin. I said good morning Kaitlin what's up, she said I saw your white mommy leaving your room last night. So, I know your fucking my mother so unless you want me to tell my father, you will fuck me too with your big black cock. I know it's big and hard I felt it while you slept.

I said ok, I will fuck you too. Kaitlin said I'm glad you see things my way and since you are hard, I would like my first black cock now. I said cool, turning over unto Kaitlin, she was all smiles as I took hold of my bone to penetrate her. I intentionally slammed my black cock up her white cunt. Kaitlin moaned oh my god your big, I started fucking her and she moaned with pleasure as I gave her pleasure.

I thought this is the best blackmail ever fuck me or else. I squeezed her big titties that she inherited from her hot mom, Katherine. I moaned and told Kaitlin my black dick feels so good in your little white pussy. Kaitlin said oh god your big cock is wonderful as I felt her cream on my cock. I said damn Kaitlin you came already, she said oh yeah you have the best dick ever. I pounded her harder and harder trying to come in her when I got that great feeling and let it go. I filled Kaitlin with my love for her. I hugged her tight and kissed her. She said thanks for the cock and cream pie. I said my pleasure sexy Kaitlin.

We both heard Katherine scream breakfast is ready. We both said oh shit putting on our robes and running downstairs for breakfast. We both hugged and kissed Katherine good morning. We all sat down to eat with my sperm in both mother and daughter. I thought that was so fucking erotic. I said you both look very beautiful this morning both of them blushed turning red as we ate breakfast.

When the weekend came, Katherine asked me if I wanted to go camping and I said yeah. Kaitlin said I want to go too and Katherine said sure the more the merrier. After work on Friday, the three of us loaded up the truck and took off to the camp.

We arrived and set up the tent, its big enough to hold 4 people so three was no problem. Katherine made us dinner and we ate talking then made smores. When we got sleepy, we turned in for the evening. Kaitlin got in her sleeping bag and I got in the same sleeping bag as Katherine.

I was asleep when Katherine woke me up and said I'm horny I need you inside of me. I said but Kaitlin is right there. Katherine said please sweetheart, I really need some cock in me, I'm so wet. She took my hand and put it on her pussy. I thought wow, she is leaking. I mounted horny Katherine and penetrated her deep. I kissed her to be quiet as I slow fucked her tight little cunt. Damn what a rush to be fucking my white mommy with my white sister so close. I could feel the steam and pleasure between us as Katherine creamed my cock over and over before I filled her with my passion cream.

Katherine said thank you honey I love you and I really appreciate this more than you know. I said my pleasure Katherine always happy to please you. We kissed then cuddle before falling asleep.

When we all woke up, Katherine pulled down her nightgown before she got out of the sleeping bag. I put my boxers back on before exiting the sleeping bag. Katherine said I'll make us breakfast.

Kaitlin said hey how about some cock after Katherine left the tent. I said are you wet,

Kaitlin said I'm always wet when a big cock that I need is around. I went over to Kaitlin and shoved my cock up her cunt quickly. We kissed as I fucked Kaitlin hard and fast. I whispered oh god, so good being in you again with your mom outside. Kaitlin said such a rush that we might get caught. She moaned oh god I'm cumming on your big fucking dick. A few moments later, I filled Kaitlin with all the sperm I had left in my scrotum.

Kaitlin said oh my god that was so good thank you and I love you. I said I love you too Kaitlin. Katherine yelled that breakfast is ready. I took my cock out of Kaitlin and put on some clothes. Kaitlin exited the tent first then I came out second. We ate breakfast together laughing and joking.

All three of us went for a hike then came back. I left Katherine and Kaitlin talking and took a nap. I was asleep when I heard them both scream my name then said get the gun, a bear is coming. I got the gun quickly and came out aiming. The bear was pretty close. I aimed at the torso and fired, first shot slowed him down, second slowed him some more then the third shot put his ass down.

We gutted him and skinned him because Kent loved bear meat. We got a ton of meat for the freezer to surprise Kent when he got back from Japan. We went home shortly thereafter because we had to get the meat into the freezer before it spoiled.

The next Saturday, I was on the couch with Katherine and Kaitlin late at night waiting for a call from Kent. Katherine whispered in my ears that Kaitlin isn't wearing any panties. I looked at Kaitlin then looked between her sweet white thighs and smiled. She made no attempts to close those sweet white thighs as I enjoyed the erotic view.

I whispered to Katherine damn your daughters vagina looks so beautiful, its making my black cock rock hard. Katherine said oh yeah, I can see the bulge now I'm going to get wet.

Kaitlin said what are you two whispering back and forth about. Katherine said your brother can see your bare white vagina, where is your panties missy. Kaitlin said I didn't feel like wearing panties, I'm sure it's not the first white vagina that he has seen. I said it's not the first white vagina that I've seen, Kaitlin said see and I don't care if he sees my white vagina.

Katherine said but you are going to make his black penis hard. Kaitlin took her t-shirt off and said this should make him even harder revealing her big tits too. Katherine said oh my god you're so naughty making your black brother hard like this.

Katherine’s phone rang and it was Kent. She said hello baby how is Japan. He said great how is everyone doing. I said I’m fine and Kaitlin said she is fine too. I said she is very fine, Katherine giggled then said we got you some bear meat. Kent said oh god that is great, I can’t wait to get home and eat some off the grill.

I took my dick out and Kaitlin started to finger her pussy as I stroked my cock. Katherine said say hello to Ichika and Akira for me. They said goodbye. Kaitlin and I asked who is Ichika and Akira.

Katherine moved my hand off my cock and stroked it as Kaitlin’s eyes got wide. She said Ichika is your daddy’s girlfriend in Japan and Akira is your half-brother. Kaitlin said oh my god mom and you’re ok with that happening.

Katherine said your dad and I made a deal Kaitlin that if I take our black son as a lover to satisfy my black craving while he satisfies his Japanese woman craving, its ok.

I said wow this is so interesting. Kaitlin said I have a confession. I blackmailed my black brother into fucking me and I feel bad about it. I said its ok Kaitlin I enjoyed every second of being inside of you. Katherine said I know you saw me leaving your black brothers room naked after he fucked me from the cameras.

Kaitlin said oops damn hallway camera, Katherine and I started laughing. Kaitlin said not funny. She got up ripped my pants off and slid down my black pole as her mom watched. I moaned deep in Kaitlin and she said oh my god yes. Katherine said you love his big black penis don't you girl. Kaitlin said fuck yeah, I love his big dick and Katherine said me too honey.

The end

www.ingramcontent.com/pod-product-compliance
Lightning Source LLC
LaVergne TN
LVHW020545160826
845677LV00015B/4205

9798848605884